Dedalus Europe
General Editor: Timothy Lane

FISH LETTERS
(AND OTHER STORIES)

GODERDZI CHOKHELI

FISH LETTERS
(AND OTHER STORIES)

edited by
Lia Chokoshvili

with an introduction by
Geoffrey Gosby and an afterword by
Ollie Matthews

translated by
Clifford Marcus, Ollie Matthews
and Walker Thompson

Dedalus

ARTS COUNCIL ENGLAND
Supported using public funding by

Published in the UK by Dedalus Limited,
24-26, St Judith's Lane, Sawtry, Cambs, PE28 5XE
info@dedalusbooks.com
www.dedalusbooks.com

ISBN printed book 978 1 915568 67 0
ISBN ebook 978 1 915568 87 8

Dedalus is distributed in the USA & Canada by SCB Distributors
15608 South New Century Drive, Gardena, CA 90248
info@scbdistributors.com   www.scbdistributors.com

Dedalus is distributed in Australia by Peribo Pty Ltd
58, Beaumont Road, Mount Kuring-gai, N.S.W. 2080
info@peribo.com.au   www.peribo.com.au

First published by Dedalus in 2025
Fish Letters copyright © *Nino Melashvili-Chokheli 1986*
Translation copyright © *Clifford Marcus, Ollie Matthews and Walker Thompson 2025*
Introduction copyright © *Geoffrey Gosby 2025*
Afterword copyright © *Ollie Matthews 2025*

The right of Nino Melashvili-Chokheli to be identified as the author and Clifford Marcus, Ollie Matthews, and Walker Thompson as the translators of this work has been asserted by them in accordance with the Copyright, Designs and Patents Act, 1988.

Printed and bound in the UK by Clays Elcograf S.p.A.
Typeset by Marie Lane

This book is sold subject to the condition that it shall not, by way of trade or otherwise, be lent, resold, hired out or otherwise circulated without the publisher's prior consent in any form of binding or cover other than that in which it is published and without a similar condition including this condition being imposed on the subsequent purchaser.

A C.I.P. listing for this book is available on request.

THE AUTHOR
GODERDZI CHOKHELI

Goderdzi Chokheli was born in 1954 in a small village northeast of Tbilisi, and died in Tbilisi in 2007. He was one of the most important filmmakers and prose writers of his era. He published one novel, *Human Sadness*, as well as a collection of short stories and some poetry. His films and screenplays won many awards both inside Georgia and abroad. In 1982 he was awarded the Grand Prize at the Oberhausen International Short Film Festival for his film *Adgilis deda*.

His unique place in Georgian society and culture is encapsulated by Levan Berdzenishvili: "Goderdzi Chokheli did not write anti-Soviet literature, he wrote non-Soviet literature. This is something that nobody else was able to do."

THE EDITOR
LIA CHOKOSHVILI

LIA CHOKOSHVILI has been teaching Georgian at the University of Oxford for twenty-seven years. The Georgian Department at Oxford is funded by the Marjory Wardrop Fund which was set up in the early twentieth century by the British diplomat Sir Oliver Wardrop to promote the study and teaching of Georgian. Both Oliver and his sister Marjory were translators so setting up a translation project in 2015 with her more advanced students seemed particularly appropriate to Lia. Since then, the Oxford Georgian Translation Project has published translations of seminal works of Georgian literature, including Goderdzi Chokheli's novel, *Human Sadness* (Dedalus, 2024). Information about the project can be found at: https://areastudies.web.ox.ac.uk/the-oxford-georgian-translation-project-continuing-the-wardrops-legacy.

THE TRANSLATORS & CONTRIBUTORS

GEOFFREY GOSBY completed his doctoral thesis on Georgian linguistics in 2017. His translations from Georgian to English include *The Man in the Panther's Skin: A Condensed Prose Retelling* (2018), *The State Controller's Office of the Democratic Republic of Georgia* (2020) and *Life in Soviet Georgia: 70 Stories* (2021). As a member of the Oxford Georgian Translation Project he has already contributed to the translation of *Stories from Saba: Selected Tales from the Book of Wisdom and Lies* (2023) and is currently translating Sulkhan-Saba Orbeliani's *Journey to Europe*.

CLIFFORD MARCUS works as a translator mainly in the field of Life Sciences. His first degree was in PPE at Oxford and he has MAs in Italian and Classics from Indiana University. He has been studying Georgian since 2012 and been involved in several Georgian literary translation projects, including *Unlocking the Door* (2017) and stories by Goderdzi Chokheli. He divides his time between Tallinn, Estonia and Oxford, England.

OLLIE MATTHEWS took up Georgian lessons whilst reading French and Russian at Jesus College, Oxford. He has been a member of the Oxford Georgian Translation Project since its inception. His translations have appeared in *Unlocking the Door* (2017) and *Stories from Saba: Selected Tales from The Book of Wisdom and Lies* (2023). He is one of the translators of Goderdzi Chokheli's *Human Sadness* (Dedalus, 2024). He is an aspiring novelist and short-story writer. His travel writing can be found on his blog Follow the Dragon.

WALKER THOMPSON read Russian and German as an undergraduate at Magdalen College, Oxford, before going on to obtain a Master's in Syriac Studies at Wolfson College. From 2019-2024, he worked in various capacities at the Institute for Slavic Studies of Heidelberg University, where he completed his doctorate in Slavic Philology in March 2024. He has been actively involved in translation projects at Oxford since 2016 and is a contributor to the Georgian-English translation of *Unlocking the Door* (2017).

CONTENTS

INTRODUCTION	by Geoffrey Gosby	**11**
FISH LETTERS	translated by Walker Thompson	**19**
CIPOLLINO	translated by Walker Thompson	**43**
FULL STOP AND COMMA	translated by Ollie Matthews	**55**
NINE QUESTIONS ABOUT LOVE	translated by Clifford Marcus	**63**
THE COMMUNAL CROW	translated by Ollie Matthews	**75**
AFTERWORD	by Ollie Matthews	**85**

"A Godforsaken Gorge":
The World of Goderdzi Chokheli

Follow the River Mtkvari northward through Tbilisi to Georgia's ancient capital, Mtskheta, and you will find the point where it is joined by the clear waters of the River Aragvi. Continue along the banks of the Aragvi up into the southern slopes of the Greater Caucasus mountain range, to the Zhinvali Reservoir and then further north-eastward, and you will come to the town of Pasanauri, where the Aragvi forks into two tributaries: the Mtiuleti Aragvi, also known as the "White Aragvi", to the northwest and the Gudamaqari Aragvi, also known as the "Black Aragvi", to the northeast. Follow the latter, keeping northwest, and not far from its source on Mount Chaukhi, you will come to the village of Chokhi in the historical northeast Georgian region of Gudamaqari, birthplace of Goderdzi Chokheli and the setting behind much of his work. These Georgian highlands—in which, together with Gudamaqari, the prominent neighbouring historical regions of Pshavi, Khevi, Mtiuleti, Khevsureti and Tusheti can also be found—occupy a special place in Georgian history, and accordingly, in Georgian culture, having existed largely beyond the influence of the Georgian state, yet have acted at

INTRODUCTION

various times as its protector and refuge.

The eleventh-century chronicler Leonti Mroveli mentions the Gudamaqarians, together with the Pkhovians, or present-day Pshavians and Khevsuretians, in his *The Lives of the Georgian Kings* (*Mepeta Tskhovreba*) among the "mountaineers" to whom St. Nino unsuccessfully preached Christianity at Tsobeni following her conversion of King Mirian III of Iberia in the fourth century. Subsequently, we are told, the *eristavi* accompanying her "victoriously destroyed their idols", since which, of the mountaineers, "some remain heathens to this day".[1] That Christianity has taken on its own shape here in the centuries since under the influence of local pre-Christian beliefs is illustrated by the traditions surrounding St. George, the revered protector of Georgia whose feast day St. Nino—by legend, his relative—is believed to have instituted. *Giorgoba*, which is celebrated on 23rd November, commemorates St. George's martyrdom, including his torture on the wheel, by the emperor Diocletian in 303 A.D. In one Gudamaqarian version, St. George was attached to a cartwheel by his fellow Tatars after preaching to them and rolled down from a high mountain, causing him to be cut into three hundred and sixty-three pieces, the landing site of each of which is marked by a shrine. The shrine (*khati*, a term which otherwise denotes a Christian icon) of St. George in Goderdzi Chokheli's home village of Chokhi marks the landing site of his tongue, and tradition has it that St. George "follows the tongue", so that—as we learn about in Chokhi's novel *Human Sadness* (*Adamianta Sevda*)[2]—no

---

[1] Mroveli, L., *The Lives of the Georgian Kings*. In: Jones, S. (Ed.), *Kartlis Tskhovreba: A History of Georgia*. Artanuji Publishing, 2014, p.65
[2] Chokheli, G., *Human Sadness*. Dedalus, 2024

INTRODUCTION

Chokhian should be refused a woman's hand in marriage for fear of her being cursed,[3] while the nearby shrine of Pirimze Pudzis Angelozi is held to be the landing site of St. George's arm, thereby accounting for the many fights that have broken out among its visitors.[4] Not far from the first of the two shrines are two boulders that are associated with three *devis*—ogre-like beings from Georgian mythology—believed to have been pressed into service by St. George as bailiffs, where visitors to the shrine have traditionally slaughtered livestock as an offering to them.[5]

Where Christianity had difficulty penetrating, the Georgian state in its various manifestations did as well. The Duchy of Aragvi (1335-1743), itself resistant to royal domination, succeeded eventually in bringing Mtiuleti, Gudamaqari, and

---

3 Alaverdashvili, K., *"tsminda giorgistan dakavshirebuli salocavebi gudamaqarshi, khevsa da tushetshi"* [Shrines Connected with St. George in Gudamakari, Khevi, and Tusheti]. In: Ghambashidze, N. and Alaverdashvili, K., *aghmosavlet sakartvelos mtianetis tradiciuli kultura (gudamaqris, khevis, tushetis salocavebi)* [Traditional Culture of the East Georgian Highlands (The Shrines of Gudamakari, Khevi, and Tusheti)]. Meridiani, 2018, pp.329-330

4 Ghambashidze, N., *"gudamaqari: pirimze pudzis angelozi—gudamaqris mtavari salocavi"* [Gudamaqari: Pirimze Pudzis Angelozi—the Main Shrine of Gudamaqari]. In: Ghambashidze, N. and Alaverdashvili, K., *aghmosavlet sakartvelos mtianetis tradiciuli kultura (gudamaqris, khevis, tushetis salocavebi)* [Traditional Culture of the East Georgian Highlands (The Shrines of Gudamakari, Khevi, and Tusheti)]. Meridiani, 2018, pp.42-43

5 Alaverdashvili, K., *"tsminda giorgistan dakavshirebuli salocavebi gudamaqarshi, khevsa da tushetshi"* [Shrines Connected with St. George in Gudamakari, Khevi, and Tusheti]. In: Ghambashidze, N. and Alaverdashvili, K., *aghmosavlet sakartvelos mtianetis tradiciuli kultura (gudamaqris, khevis, tushetis salocavebi* [Traditional Culture of the East Georgian Highlands (The Shrines of Gudamakari, Khevi, and Tusheti)]. Meridiani, 2018, pp.329-330

INTRODUCTION

Khevi under its control, only to succumb to a revolt of its peasant subjects in which the last of the dukes, Bezhan, was killed; meanwhile, Pshavi and Khevsureti resisted incorporation and remained territories that answered directly to the Georgian crown. This resistance to the close control of the state and its feudal system is reflected in the traditional social organisation of the highland regions into *temis*, individual communities led by a *khevisberi* ("gorge elder") who performed the roles of chief, priest, and military leader, and whose title is mentioned in the legal code instituted in the fourteenth century by Giorgi V the Brilliant in an attempt to impose regulation on the blood law and other highland customs that he observed among the Mtiuletian tribes.[6] While their beliefs and customs may have differed from those of other Georgians, however, the Georgian highlanders did not hesitate to confront the common enemy, whether this was the Muslim Kists (a historical term for the Nakh peoples, including the Chechens and Ingush) with whom they shared a frequently violent coexistence at Georgia's borders, or those from further afield. When Agha Mohammed Khan invaded and sacked Tbilisi in 1795 in retribution for Erekle II's signing of the Treaty of Giorgievsk with Imperial Russia, it was three hundred warriors from the banks of the Aragvi (the majority of whom, according to the Chokhian chronicler Samkharauli in *Human Sadness*, were Gudamaqarians) who fought a heroic last stand at the capital and allowed the king to retreat up the Aragvi valley, where the pursuing Iranians were stopped by another three hundred warriors (in this case, Khevsuretians) and Erekle II was able

---

6 Dolidze, I.S., *kartuli samartlis dzeglebi tom.* [Monuments of Georgian Law Vol. 1]. Tbilisi, 1963, pp.401-21

INTRODUCTION

to take refuge in a highland fortress.[7]

The harsh frontier existence of the Georgian highlanders and their rigid social code inspired a wealth of folk poetry, upon which major figures in Georgian literature in turn drew from in the nineteenth and the twentieth centuries, including Aleksandre Qazbegi, Mikhail Javakhishvili, and perhaps most significantly, Vazha Pshavela, who, writing primarily of life in Khevsureti and Pshavi, "turns this heroic lost world into a golden age which is approaching its end; at the same time it stands at the dawn of humanity, its heroes Promethean battlers against cruel gods".[8] In such poems as "Aluda Ketelauri" (*Aluda Ketelauri*, 1888), "Guest and Host" (*Stumar-Maspindzeli*, 1893), and "The Snake-Eater" (*Gvelis Mchameli*, 1901), we find a preoccupation in his poetry with the inevitability of the individual and their ideals succumbing to the unstoppable forces of nature, including human nature in the form of the *temi* and its unbending traditions.[9] In "Aluda Ketelauri", Aluda is banished when his own morals prevent him from following the laws of his community and cutting off the right hand of an Ingush tribesman who he has killed, while in "Guest and Host", the resistance mounted by the Chechen Joqola to his fellow villagers, who slay a Khevsur to whom he had mistakenly offered his hospitality, result in his and his family's banishment. The hero of "The Snake-Eater", Mindia, obtains magical powers to communicate with the natural world, only to be forced to forfeit them by his need to do violence to

---

7 Rayfield, D., *Edge of Empires: A History of Georgia*. Reaktion Books, 2012, pp.255-256
8 Rayfield, D., *The Literature of Georgia: A History* (3rd ed.). Garnett Press, 2010, p.218
9 Ibid., pp.207-216

INTRODUCTION

that same world in order to provide for his family. Such stories were being told in an age when, as discussed by Manning (2012),[10] Georgia was experiencing a broader ethnographic and literary "turn towards the mountains". In Ilia Chavchavadze's *A Traveller's Essays* (*Mgzavris Tserilebi*), first published in 1871, a young student recounts a stretch of a journey home from his studies in St. Petersburg to Tbilisi which takes him from Vladikavkaz across the River Terek (Chavchavadze and others of his time who were among the first Georgians to study in Russia were called the *Tergdaleulebi*, or "those who have drunk from the Terek") and down—presumably following the Gudamaqari Aragvi's sister tributary, the Mtiuleti Aragvi—towards the same town of Pasanauri, from which his route to the capital would have been as described above. On the way, his sense of Georgianness is redefined as he discovers common ground with Lelt Ghunia, a local mountain guide who initially appears quite foreign to him.

Though Chokheli writes of the Georgian highlands in the late twentieth century, in his work we encounter traditions and symbols similar to those found in Vazha Pshavela and his contemporaries; in *Human Sadness*, for example, there is often mortal conflict with the Kists across the frontier, the practice of severing the right hands of defeated enemies, and the tragic spectacle of the once-proud eagle brought low (see Vazha Pshavela's poem "The Eagle", *Artsivi*, 1887). And, though they take place in the Soviet context of Chokheli's time, and are related with Chokheli's unique blend of humour

---

10 Manning, P., *Strangers in a Strange Land: Occidentalist Publics and Orientalist Geographies in Nineteenth-Century Georgian Imaginaries*. Academic Studies Press, 2012, pp.28-58

INTRODUCTION

and philosophy, the conflicts that we encounter in the short stories "Cipollino" (*Chipolino*) and "Fish Letters" (*Tevzis Tserilebi*) in particular are reminiscent of those faced by the like of Aluda Ketelauri, Joqola and Mindia. In this primeval Georgia, the individual remains torn between the captivity of human existence and the possibility of freedom.

Geoffrey Gosby

FISH LETTERS

translated by Walker Thompson

"The soul has no beginning and no end," Gamikhardai said to me the day before yesterday, and left me.

The day before that I had been asking people about the existence of the soul, but he hadn't said anything to me then. "I don't know," he said with a shrug; he had said this just yesterday morning. He didn't say anything else and rushed off to do the scything. As he was in a rush, he left his knapsack with his packed lunch at home, and his own little girl ran after him with it along the road.

It wasn't even light outside yet. At the top of an alleyway between two houses, the foreman appeared and accosted Gamikhardai: "Gamikhardai, where are you going, eh?"

"To do the scything."

"No, not the scything; you're going to shear the lambs."

"But who will do the scything for me? You know I'm the

FISH LETTERS

only hand around."

"Cut the talk," the foreman said to him with the voice of a man supremely confident in himself and started off towards me.

Gamikhardai turned his back to him and didn't go to shear sheep, but rather set off downhill towards the hayfield.

"Gamikhardai!" the foreman screamed at him. "Where are you going, eh?"

"To work!" Gamikhardai shouted back down at him and continued along his way.

"You'll pay for this!" the foreman shouted and then turned towards me.

"Don't come up again today to write. Got it?"

"Why?" I asked.

"Why? Because you are wasting people's time with your questions."

I had been going up to the sheep shearing for two days and asking about the existence of the soul. Two days earlier, I asked Gamikhardai, too, but he didn't say anything to me then. Gamikhardai is an honest man; my fellow-villagers call him a wretch, because he lives poorly and ekes out an honest living for himself and his several children. This morning, I felt sorry for him for some reason; I'm not sure whether it was because he left his bread at home, or because his daughter came running after him... I don't know, I don't know... he was walking up and putting foot to ground as if his body were alien upon this earth and he thus felt uncomfortable setting foot on it.

"Yesterday the commandant also got cross with you," the foreman said.

FISH LETTERS

"What do you think? Where does the soul go?" I said.

"I don't think anything," he said to me and suddenly started getting ready to go.

"Does the soul die?"

"What soul? Which soul? What are you on about?"

"The soul that's inside every person—that one."

"There's nothing inside people," he said. "We come into the world and we die. That's it."

"That's it, and nothing more?"

"I don't have time for you now and I don't want to see you coming up there," he said and called back to Gamikhardai as the latter was walking up: "I'll see you at the hayfield!"

"What's your problem with him?"

"That he isn't coming to the sheep shearing."

"What does it matter if he isn't coming? He's working!"

"What work is he doing?"

"Scything, sweeping, making hay bales."

"We'll see about that tomorrow," he said and set off towards the middle of the village.

* * *

Yesterday was Sunday. Gamikhardai spent all day working, carrying hay bales down onto the floodplain, with his wife and children helping.

It was hot. Dust rose up from the earth as they dragged the hay bales along. His children were covered in dirt.

In the evening, they brought in the hay and sat down to eat bread by a spring.

Several trucks appeared down below, turned off the road

FISH LETTERS

and stopped by the haystacks.

"Is this all your hay?" the foreman asked Gamikhardai, who was holding a dry bread crust in his hand.

"Yes, it is."

"You don't have any more?"

"No, no more."

"How many are there?"

"Thirty."

"You have to give us twenty-five."

"How so, twenty-five, when the quota says fifteen?"

"It says fifteen, but you've been put down for twenty-five because you didn't come to the sheep shearing."

"How can I provide for myself with five bales? It won't even feed one cow. And what about the children?"

"What they told you—that's how it is," the foreman said, and the cars pulled up to the haystacks. The workmen left five haystacks behind and got into their cars.

Gamikhardai was in shock and trembling, now looking at his children, then at the trucks. He was shaking all over.

"Let's go," the foreman said. The trucks started their engines, loudly.

Gamikhardai sat there at a loss for words, shaking. He took a match from his pocket, went up to one of the hay bales, and struck the match.

"What are you doing? No!" his wife cried.

"Get off me!" Gamikhardai pushed his wife away and tossed the lit match onto the haystack.

"You worked all summer and now you are burning it?" his wife said, gripping him. The woman took off her veil and started to snuff out the flames, but it was too late: the dry

FISH LETTERS

haystack caught fire and the yellow tongues of flame licked up into the air in five places.

Gamikhardai's wife was standing there dishevelled and weeping. The children were embracing her and gripping the hem of her skirt.

Gamikhardai was standing there and watching the fire. Then he glanced at the trucks departing down the hill and set off running down head-over-heels towards them.

He was running as fast as he could towards the Aragvi. His wife gave chase, followed by his children and eventually the whole village. Everyone thought he was going to drown himself.

While we were walking, he stripped off his clothes, went up to the bank of the Aragvi, and jumped into the water as naked as the day he was born. When he reached the middle, he found an eddy and sat down in it. He was holding only his head above the water and not even looking at us; he was looking up at some point in the sky.

The people were sitting by the bank of the river and waiting for Gamikhardai to come out onto the bank. But Gamikhardai had no intention of doing this.

"Let's go: maybe we're embarrassing him," the priest said, and took the others with him.

Gamikhardai's wife and children remained there. I sat down on a stone some distance away.

"Don't you have to come out?" his wife called out. He didn't make a sound. Then his wife began to beg him. Gamikhardai didn't budge. The children began to cry.

He sat there, motionless, in one place, until the evening. At sunset, the village people gathered at the riverbank. They were calling to Gamikhardai: "Come out! Enough sitting in the water! You'll catch a cold and die!" He didn't even look at them, not even once; he acted as if he couldn't hear their voices.

Gamikhardai's wife and children were pouring forth tears in floods.

Everybody had come down from the village to the Aragvi. The commandant of the collective farm came at last and shouted to Gamikhardai, "You useless lump! Come out onto the bank at once!"

He, however, paid no heed.

"What are we talking so much for? Let's go and drag him out," the foreman said and got into the water. Several men followed him in.

Gamikhardai followed the course of the river and stopped right before the top of a waterfall. If he had gone just a little bit further downstream, that would have been the end of it. The men were still walking towards him, but when Gamikhardai started to move slowly downstream, they became afraid, saying, "Won't he fall in?" and backed away.

Dusk fell. The people started gradually to make their way back to the village.

"He'll get bored of it and then he'll come out on his own," Gabriel said.

"Let's go. Leave him alone. When night falls, he'll come out in the dark; perhaps he is ashamed now," the commandant said to the people. They led Gamikhardai's wife and children back to the village, too, saying, "If he doesn't see you there any more, he'll be more likely to come out."

That night was so dark that nothing was visible. Only the

sound of the Aragvi reached the village.

The next morning, the people gathered at the bank of the Aragvi. Gamikhardai had come halfway out of the water and was shivering. When he saw the people, he sat down so that he was up to his neck in the water.

"Don't you have to come out?" his wife asked him, weeping.

"He's wasting people's time, the son of a…" raged the foreman. "Not only are you not working, but you're wasting people's time, too! If you don't get out, I'll call the police," the commandant yelled and added, "I'll count to five and then you'd better get out fast!"

Gamikhardai didn't even look at them. He was gazing at the sun and thinking, "When will it come up?" It was as if he felt cold.

After half an hour, they brought the police.

"Won't he come out?" the police officer asked without prompting.

Gamikhardai paid no heed.

"Will you come out or do I have to come in?" he repeated the question, but since he couldn't get an answer, he resolved to go in.

Gamikhardai shifted down towards the waterfall and the people held the policeman back.

"If you don't come out, we'll put you away for five years," the policeman raged.

But Gamikhardai paid no heed.

"Five years for not heeding the people's requests and making an absurd spectacle of yourself, plus one year will be added for indecent exposure in a public place, and two years

FISH LETTERS

for running away from your wife and children and causing them to suffer, and three years for wasting people's time, and one and a half more so far for disobeying my orders."

The policeman fired his revolver into the air, but Gamikhardai was acting as if nothing was going on.

The sun came up and Gamikhardai stared greedily at it. We left him alone.

"If he comes out, he'll come out faster without us," the commandant said. "Let's bring his wife and children back home."

* * *

At home, I wrote a letter on paper to Gamikhardai:

GAMIKHARDAI—

Why won't you come out? Why won't you make a sound? Do you not feel sorry for your wife and children? Surely you are not the sort of person to act on impulses, who fancies a sit in the water and goes ahead and sits there.

Let me know what the matter is.
—LUKA

* * *

I wrapped up the letter in several other pieces of paper, put a pen inside, and dropped it off in the whirlpool for Gamikhardai. He looked all around, and when he saw I was the only one there, he opened my letter and read it, but did not make a sound. He picked up the pen and wrote to me:

FISH LETTERS

From this day on, I shall not have anything more to do with men. I do not wish to live as a man in a place where justice is not served, where labour is not valued, and where a person is not treated as a person. I used to love people, but I do not love them any longer. I do not love them anymore because I am no longer a man.

I am a fish!

I do not want to have anything at all in common with people anymore. I will forget you all—and what wife and children are you talking about? The ones who are weeping over me because I am in the water? Yes, you are right! I did once have a wife and children, but that was before, when I was a human being, back then. Even two days ago, if you like. But today, I am a fish and I have nothing whatsoever in common with you all!

This is my desire.

—A FISH

* * *

GAMIKHARDAI—

You say you are a fish, but this is not so. We know full well you are a man. How could you forget your past entirely? Do you really expect anyone to believe you? No matter how much you try, you will never become a fish. In what way do you look like a fish? Just because you are in the water?

No, you are not a fish and you cannot be one. This is absurd. It is better for you to return soon to society, to your wife and kids, to earth.

FISH LETTERS

Aren't you hungry?
—LUKA

* * *

I am not hungry. I am not hungry yet.

As for society, people, the earth—they don't exist for me anymore. I have forsaken everybody and everything.

I cannot remember anymore: was I ever really a man?

I am a fish now. How good it is to be a fish! It is a completely different world here. The world of people is a dog-eat-dog world. And you are so wedded to the idea of being a person! So that if somebody tells you that you are not a person, it would cause you to die this very minute. Often, you have a hard time as a human being, but you don't have enough strength to refuse to be this way.

I wonder whether any of you ever dreamt of being a fish.

I know you often dream of being a bird. That's how you escape the human condition.

Hmm...?
—A FISH

* * *

GAMIKHARDAI—

When we dream of turning into a bird, about flying just once, we are not escaping the fact of being human! No! Right at that moment, we especially love being human, we dream of flying in order to make human existence more beautiful, to discover greater freedom through flight.

FISH LETTERS

Is the world of people a dog-eat-dog world?

You may be right. Wasn't it you yourself who fled from the struggle?

You couldn't cope with human difficulties and it was for this reason that you have set yourself apart from us. Look into your heart: if someone runs away from the human condition because of difficulties, will things work out for him as a fish?

Do you really think that fish have it easy?

Why do they not come up onto dry land when the river turns rough in a flood?

Of course, fish also eat one another in the water.

For the time being, they are afraid of you and perhaps they aren't even coming close to you. This is because you are stronger than they are. If, however, they sense weakness, they will chew you to bits, so that all that will be left of you is your bones. So shout at them as much as you want, saying, "I am a fish! I am a fish!"

So it's better if you get out on time; otherwise, I think that what I said is bound to happen.

You shouldn't run away from people, no, you shouldn't.
—LUKA

* * *

First of all, given that I am a fish and not Gamikhardai, as you have been writing to me, what sort of freedom can you be talking about? You want to be free and thus dream about being a bird? If you people love one another, then why do you enslave one another? You do not love freedom, but rather love enslaving and debasing each other. You are right: I couldn't

FISH LETTERS

cope with the difficulties of being human and turned into a fish. But then again, what is wrong with this?

I want to be a fish.

Things won't work out for me as a fish? So what? I will die this way, as I want, as a fish.

I do not fear death. Human beings are afraid of death; I am not.

Why am I not afraid?

Because the soul doesn't have a beginning or an end.

—A FISH

* * *

It may be that the soul doesn't have a beginning or an end, but it is obvious that the soul that is in a human being cannot become a fish's soul. The body is made of matter, and matter has a form, and this form is subject to time. A soul can pass through several bodies, but these bodies, as the rule says, must leave their own imprint on the soul. Therefore, it might be possible for the soul of a man to come to dwell in a fish, but I don't think it is. This means (if it is indeed true!) that the soul together with the body completes its own existence. Otherwise, the soul continues to exist, but it has to remember—and if a human soul remembers, then it remains a human soul and continues to be human even without being material. This means that you can in no case be a fish. Wishing you were a fish is one thing, and actually being one is another.

Isn't being human difficult? Yes, you are right. It is difficult, very difficult, but if we all got in the water and shouted that we're fish, like you, what would come of it? We'd all start

FISH LETTERS

attacking one another, and it would be curious to see where you'd run away to—maybe then you'd say 'no' to being a fish.

It would be best if you came back. Do you not see your children crying?

—LUKA

* * *

The soul has the right to choose whatever it desires.

You can't deny me this.

My soul doesn't want to be among men, and I have every right to be a fish.

It's possible for the soul to forget, isn't it?

I will forget about men. That's it.

—A FISH

* * *

You won't be able to forget about men. Your soul will always remember moments full of human joys and sorrows.

Your soul will always remember the sweet melancholy of solitude.

Your soul will always remember human sin and grace.

Your soul will always remember God, in Whom you believed, or, if you did not believe in Him, at least you had Him in your being.

Your soul will always remember the people you had around you.

Your soul will always remember the ground you walked on.

Your soul will always remember the things to which you

FISH LETTERS

have grown accustomed.

In your soul, there will always be a fear: the fear of nonexistence.

And who knows how many other things besides...?

Who knows? In a week's time, hunger may force you back to the world of men. And you soul will remember this, too, for a long time.

Your children send their regards.

We are waiting for you.

—LUKA

* * *

I count as nought all those minutes full of human joy and sorrow.

We fish can experience solitude, as well.

God is within us as much as within human beings.

We fish love one another. We love the water more than you love the land, for the sake of which you devour one another.

The fear of nonexistence? Do you really presume that only you people have this fear?

Regardless of how hungry I might be, I shall not return to the world of men.

Did I have children? I don't remember.

I have decided to have children here. What is left for me back in your world?

You can have your land and your food and your drink—just leave me alone. Don't stop me from forgetting.

—A FISH

* * *

FISH LETTERS

For the third day in a row, the village gathered together at the banks of the River Aragvi. Some people proposed one thing, others something else.

"If you don't get out of there in two days, I will have to file a complaint about you!" the foreman shouted to Gamikhardai. "I'll have to expel you from the collective farm, because you are wasting people's time!" He didn't make a sound, as if he couldn't hear.

Once again, the police came to threaten to take a statement from the "fish". In response, he shifted further downstream towards the waterfall.

Nothing got through to him, and he wasn't listening to anyone. He just went underwater from time to time.

That night, the moon was shining brightly across the whole locality, and the people saw a little girl standing at the water's edge, begging Gamikhardai: "Daddy, come out! Just come out, and I'll never make you angry anymore! I'll buy you some sweets. Don't be a fish, I'm begging you!"

When she saw that her entreaties were of no effect, she went back to the village in tears.

That night, the people protested. They got together and told me, "Write a letter in the morning saying that if he doesn't get out, we will be forced to banish him according to the old rules."

"My dear good people," his wife begged them, "Don't ruin me! Just wait for now. Maybe he'll calm down, you damned idiots, eh?"

"Let's give him one more day, but after that, this simply can't go on. If he doesn't have any need for us, how much more

FISH LETTERS

can we keep on begging him?" said Deacon Mtsaria.[11] He then turned to me and said: "Write to him in the morning, and if he doesn't come out by midday, I will gather the people together and we will banish him. Who has ever heard of a human being not wanting to be a human being? That's blasphemy and nothing else. Who gave him the right to make a mockery of the people and to get ahead of himself? In spite of everything, how can he deny that he is human? What are we, then? Nothing! As if that weren't enough, how dare he make a mockery of God! If He had wanted, would it have been difficult for Him to have created him as a fish, or what? Isn't a fish simpler to create? Phooey! Let the very mention of this man be cursed! Why, God, didst Thou bring together this man's bones and breathe Thy Holy Spirit into this ingrate?"

Mtsaria fumed for a long time while the people listened.

The following morning, I wrote a letter to Gamikhardai:

My dear Fish—

You are offending people with your behaviour. By denying that you are human, you are causing others to lose faith. Moreover, you are having a psychological effect on society. Like it or not, you are on everyone's mind.

What do you think? It can't be easy for them to forget about you and not to think about you at all. If you were mad, it would be another matter, but as it is, you are in your right mind.

To think how your little girl was begging you last night to come out. Our hearts all burned within us, but you didn't make a sound.

---

11 Literally: "sharp-tongue".

FISH LETTERS

The people are incensed and have charged me with conveying to you that if you do not come back to the world of men by midday, they will banish you. If you say 'no', just don't forget that they have self-respect, too.

Aren't you afraid of them? When winter comes and it gets cold, you will have to come out. Otherwise, you will freeze.

Or if they banish you, whom can you turn to?

Have a think about it. You have until noon.

—LUKA

* * *

At last you have realized? Banishing people is an age-old human tactic—and, by the way, fish have no such laws.

I have rejected you already and you took it as an insult. O how vainglorious you are! You are threatening me with things of which I am not afraid! Banishment even empowers me, because it will help me to forget about you. Well done—well thought—maybe now you'll leave me be.

"The people are incensed?" How amusing! Who knows how many people have banished their fellow men and how often they have been in the right?

Am I afraid of winter? Not at all. Little by little, I will get used to living in the water as a fish. By autumn, I will have learnt how to dive and I will follow the course of the river to warmer climes. But as for you—you can act as you wish. I rejected human beings before they could reject me; that's why I'm not afraid of being banished.

—A FISH

* * *

FISH LETTERS

I read the Fish's letter to the people. A dreadful commotion broke out and they assembled at the community's gathering place on the hill. They hadn't congregated at that place in a long time. The proof of this came from the terrible stone markers with the names of exiles on them which barely could be seen protruding out of the earth, toothlike and blackened by candle-soot.

Who knows how many people had been banned there. And then what an awful word it was that they said: "Banish him!"

"People, do you see, the earth is piling up?" Mtsaria said, laying his hand upon the soil between the stones.

They got some candles and Mtsaria lit them.

The people remained completely still as they waited for the fury to begin, and in the silence his voice sounded like the sifting of sand:

"O God! Thou art glorified!

O God! Thou art to be remembered!

A man whom Thou didst fashion hath renounced his humanity and is offending the people, and hath rejected Thee likewise!

Do not be upset with us, O Thou who art good, not count us as ungrateful!

From this day on, nobody shall make mention of Gamikhardai among men.

Nobody shall say a word to him, nor shall anyone light a candle for him.

Nobody shall open the doors of their house to him.

Nobody shall hand a piece of bread to him.

FISH LETTERS

From this day, let him be banished by us!"

"Amen!" the people shouted.

"Let God's wrath descend upon this oath breaker!"

"Amen!" the people bellowed.

Mtsaria placed the candle on one of the protruding stones.

The people walked down the hill murmuring.

Gamikhardai's wife followed behind weeping. Their children were clinging to the edge of her skirt.

* * *

One week has passed since Gamikhardai went into the water. My children won't leave me alone, saying, "Write to him so that he will come back!"

However much I write, he won't come out. He has stopped answering my letters. Hunger has turned him into just skin and bones. It seems he really isn't going to come out.

Last night, a thunderstorm broke and it started bucketing down.

"Maybe he'll come back owing to the danger of flash water!" they said in the village, and started looking towards the river.

Gamikhardai's wife and children besought him with tearful trepidation to come out before the river flooded. He had climbed up on top of a boulder.

All night, the river was carrying away large rocks.

* * *

FISH LETTERS

The next day, the noise of the people woke me up.

That night, the river had washed up driftwood and the whole village dispersed across the floodplain to collect it. They wouldn't give one another a chance to gather the firewood. They were holding axes and marking out logs for themselves. When somebody marked one, another person would erase his mark and make his own instead. They couldn't settle things between themselves and started attacking each other.

Gamikhardai's head was sticking out of the water and he was laughing so that I might notice. Then he wrote me this letter:

And now you will tell me that I should return to the world of men...

Just look at this humanity of yours!
—A FISH

***

I didn't write any more letters to him. At that point, it seemed to me that there was no use in standing up for humanity, but that doesn't mean that I was on Gamikhardai's side. Basically, it was not a pretty picture. Men and women were hitting each other with pieces of wood that had been washed up by the waters of the Aragvi. It was a dreadful fracas. People swearing, shifting wood from one pile to another. Then when they had had enough and they had stocked up their own share of wood, they went back to the village in silence.

That evening, it clouded over and got even darker. All night long, everything all around was rumbling. The river was

FISH LETTERS

rushing and making a terrible noise.

I don't think anyone could sleep that night.

The next morning unfolded as follows.

The rocky floodplain of the river. The charcoal-black waters of the river on the floodplain. One or two men standing here and there on the floodplain. The river had carried away overnight the wood that it had brought the night before. Not a single splinter of it was left for anyone to have. The people were standing and looking at the sites where their wood piles had been the day before and the people who had been fighting with each other were ashamed to make a sound. The fish that had washed up in the flood were lying scattered all over the plain.

Only Gamikhardai was nowhere to be seen. His wife was running dishevelled along the course of the black river, with her children running behind her, sobbing their hearts out.

This incident caused the people who had been fighting to sober up and thus brought them back together. The tragedy caused them to forget their bad feelings and they went running downriver to bring back the missing man. It was heartbreaking to watch these black-clad people racing along the seething River Aragvi, and I involuntarily thought, "Yes, it's right, it's right!" and followed on behind.

CIPOLLINO

translated by Walker Thompson

Whenever I write about my fellow villagers, I feel as if I am making a confession before Heaven and Earth.

Perhaps there is no village without an idiot. If there were such a village, full of only wise people, they would still find someone to pick on and call an "idiot", even if only because this "idiot dragged his feet when walking". You could not really even call such a man a "cripple", but each village has to have its idiot.

Alas! Even Cipollino. They called him an "idiot" in the village, and when I was a child, I, too, thought he was mad. He had no wife or children, and as I remember him, he was already past middle age. He possessed nothing apart from books, not even a cow or sheep.

"How did this poor wretch sustain himself?" I often heard people in our village ask about Cipollino. Since Cipollino didn't have any cattle or sheep, so we children believed, he lived on the air he breathed.

At the top of the village by a ruined mountain fortress there stood a birch tree. Night after night, this tree gleamed white in the dark such that you would have thought it a candle lit for prayer in a church. Amidst the branches of the tree, almost at the top, Cipollino had set up a viewing platform!

"What was he observing?" you may ask.

He was observing the stars, our dear, guileless Cipollino! He would sit there for nights on end in his lookout, which was woven together like a bird's nest, and gaze at the heavens through a pair of long, brass binoculars, whilst the stars came out, shone, and twinkled.

In the morning, Cipollino would proclaim his weather forecasts to my fellow villagers as they went out to cut hay or to do other things in the mountains. He knew the star of each of them, and if the star of any one of them portended misfortune, Cipollino would warn them on the following morning: "Your star came up very wan today, and it went down joylessly at the time of its setting. It seemed to me that it did not sing the midnight hymn together with the other stars. In these days, take heed and do not undertake anything important."

"Fine, Cipollino, fine. Really appreciate it," they would say blithely, laughing at him behind his back.

Nobody paid attention to his findings. He was universally regarded as an idiot, and no-one made much of his predictions of either the weather or of impending doom. Who knows: Cipollino may have been right, but his notions and findings were like those of a voice crying in the wilderness. His words, hurled down from the top of the birch tree, only ever grazed

CIPOLLINO

my fellow villagers' earlobes, but they never took root in them and they could not send up shoots.

I can't tell whether Cipollino could guess any of this; he was in love with what he was doing and immeasurably sincere. For him, there was no such thing as wind and rain. If anyone ever got caught outside the village at night, he wasn't afraid, as he could be sure that Cipollino would be sitting up in his tree at the top of the village. Cipollino was indeed quite similar to a night watchman. On moonlit nights, his appearance was similar to that of a bird sitting in the treetop and pointing at the sky with his brass binoculars as with a beak.

Like the whole village, Cipollino had himself forgotten his real name, yet he wasn't upset by this. Moreover, not only Cipollino, but also everyone in the village had their own nicknames, and none of them was upset by this.

In the little alleyways of our village, there could be found walking people with such names as "The Whistler" whose real name was Kako; "The Hugger" whose real name was Leo; "Government Teeth" whose real name was Petre. He had a set of false teeth and would boast that he had "government teeth" in his mouth.

On the open terraces of our village, "Hitler" would come and go. He was incredibly arrogant and adopted this name as if everybody had returned to our village from the war safe and sound.

In my village there also lived "Three-Lice". He brought this name back with him from the city. They had taken him to be operated, and when they discovered head lice and wished to get rid of them, he went mad, saying, "As if I didn't know I had them... but if they exterminate all the lice in the world, what will happen? What will you say to future generations?" When they said nothing would happen, he resorted to begging them to leave at least three for breeding. The doctor then asked whether two mightn't be enough for this purpose.

"If you leave two," he replied, "they might both be male, or else both might turn out to be female, but with a third one it's an entirely different matter—but in what you're suggesting to do, there is an element of doubt. Besides, even if you leave two and one turns out to be female and the other male, what if something bad happens beforehand? You know how the saying goes, 'Misfortune never sleeps.'"

I do not know whether they left the three lice or not, but the name "Three-Lice" stuck. He was the sort of man who didn't like to destroy any living thing. He would encounter a hunter on the road and stop him to tell him, "If you're a friend, don't shoot the hyena: there's only one or two still around and the species will die out."

"I am for the Revolution, but something has gone amiss," he would say with regret.

"Then what didn't go right?"

"The thing is that we should have left one or two feudal lords for breeding and for show, along with their estates and serfs. We should have fenced them in and kept them there. It wouldn't have taken much; what else do we have zoos for, no?"

"That wouldn't have been right," they argued with Three-Lice, "If we'd have left one or two, then the others would have wanted to stay, too, saying, 'Why us? What have we done wrong?'"

"So all we'd have to say to the others is, 'Tssst! All we

want these ones for is breeding and for show. As for you, there are plenty of things you've done wrong.'"

"But then wouldn't you feel sorry for the serfs? What did they do wrong? Everyone around them is free and they're still serfs…"

"Yes, you're right about that, I swear by the sun above me," Three-Lice said with a broken heart, and then for a long time after that he went around deep in thought.

Once "Hitler" went for a walk around an open terrace. We children were playing war and were so deeply immersed in the game that we set upon "Hitler" with sticks and cudgels. The poor man was confined to his bed for a month.

Apart from them, a "Galilei" and a "Giordano Bruno" lived in our village. This Giordano was such a stubborn man that if you had told him the Earth was turning, he would have answered, "Are you mocking me?" and probably gone mad and killed you.

Apart from them, there was an "Othello" who would pass through our village from the outside.

The local beekeeper also had a son-in-law who was called "Napoleon".

I don't know why these nicknames were so fashionable. My uncle used to say that our village is nothing, that he knows a country where some people are called "Desk", others "Inkpot", others "Aeroplane" and others still by whatever other strange names they thought up.

Evidently, this "country" my uncle had seen was not in our valley, since otherwise I would have come across either a "Desk" or an "Inkpot" somewhere. My uncle was a good liar, with all his "I know a country…" as he would say, whilst

CIPOLLINO

adding some other "Thursday lie" on top of this.

Poor Cipollino was the sole kind-hearted and noble soul to be found amongst the inhabitants of my village.

Apart from him, there was also a kind-hearted elderly woman who was nicknamed Pakhvinjeli.

Pakhvinjeli had a married kinswoman who lived in another village somewhere and came to call on her once a year. This was like Easter or a new Deluge for Pakhvinjeli. Otherwise she lived alone in her little house, which was on the brink of collapse. But this didn't bother her much; she knew the house would last her whole life and then not one stone would be left upon another. Pakhvinjeli's only livelihood and relation was an aged cow. Both of the cow's horns were broken and she had tearful eyes full of sadness. Perhaps she could sense her owner's sorrow. You could tell she was worried by the way she walked, which was different from other cows. "If an animal isn't like its owner, it's a bad sign," so it has been said, and this is very true. Animals have an impeccable intuition for their owners' thoughts, sorrows, and joys. You can meet a cow and guess whether its owner is worried or not. You can meet a horse and tell what sort of warrior its rider is, whether he is brave or cowardly. You can read it in the horse's eyes.

Pakhvinjeli's cow carried her owner's worries with her as she grazed on the meadow.

At the top of the village, there was a holy place: an icon shrine covered with a flat roof. There was a small square around the shrine, enclosed on all sides by a fence. Everybody was forbidden from crossing it, men as well as women. Only on feast days could the men traverse the square by the icon shrine. From time to time, we children would walk across the

CIPOLLINO

square to pick sour plums or wild pears, but the grown-ups would prevent us.

One evening, Pakhvinjeli's cow did not come home. The poor woman, who owing to old age was already shaking at the shoulders and knees, started to tremble even more. She was begging the grown-ups and children in turn: "May God help you, only help me somehow, people!"

Who wouldn't help an old lady? And indeed, the village spent the whole night searching for the cow by lamplight. When it got too dark to see, they called up to Cipollino in his tree: "Have you by any chance seen Pakhvinjeli's cow anywhere?"

"What would a cow be doing in the sky?" Cipollino shouted down to them.

"Nothing in the sky, but have a look around with your binoculars and you might catch a glimpse of something."

Cipollino began there and then to observe the area surrounding the village, but he too could not make out a cow. It seems that his eye, so accustomed to gazing at the sky, didn't have a sense for terrestrial things. Besides, it was night, so what would he have been able to see even if he had had a sense for it?

At daybreak, poor Pakhvinjeli, who was piteously hunched over, appeared between Heaven and Earth as a question mark partially rubbed out in the notebook of a first-year school pupil.

"Kids!" Cipollino cried out at dawn.

"Did you find her, Cipollino?" the men called.

"Send the children to look at the icon shrine—it seems the roof has collapsed."

A commotion ensued. The collapse of the roof of the

shrine was, in the eyes of my fellow villagers, not a good sign. They sent us children to see. We went, and what did we see? The eyes of Pakhvinjeli's cow staring out at us from under the roof of the collapsed icon shrine. She appeared to have been startled by wasps and to have dashed onto the roof, which gave way under her weight.

We went back down to the village and told the people. A discussion arose. Some said, "Let's go light a candle and ask the deacon to open the door of the shrine in order to let the cow out."

The deacon refused outright: "Today is not a feast day. Nothing like this ever happened when my father and grandfather were alive. It is inauspicious to open the door of the house of God before a feast."

Silence fell. Everyone was afraid to open the door on the "wrong day" and they shifted uneasily.

The old woman was leaning on her stick and looking at the men, and still resembled a question mark.

The people were right, in a way. They had a belief and were defending this belief. This belief was in their very blood, and you wouldn't have been able to break it so easily. You wouldn't have been able to smoke it out. It was a belief deep-seated not only in their mind, but also in their body: apart from on holidays, they couldn't enter the shrine or set foot in the holy place.

At the same time, they were aware of what sin and mercy are. They were also kind-hearted and felt sorry for the wretched orphan; they were eager to help her, but they could not.

There was a month left until the feast day. The cow would probably die within a month without food or water, or else a

CIPOLLINO

wild beast might come for it in the night.

The sky was above and the earth was below. Between them was suspended Pakhvinjeli, shivering and hopeless. For two to three days, the whole village was squirming uncomfortably. We children were sneaking around and we would have thrown grass down to Pakhvinjeli's cow, but the grown-ups forbade us once more.

On the third or fourth morning, the whole village woke to the sound of a cow mooing. Pakhvinjeli's cow was tied up outside her house by her harness and was mooing for her owner. The old woman rushed out, embraced the cow around the neck, and burst into sobs of joy.

The cow's eyes reflected back her owner's sorrow and joy.

The village could not forgive Cipollino for breaking down the door of the shrine. They regarded his behaviour as a kind of madness passing all limits and sought revenge on him.

At midday, when Cipollino was sleeping peacefully—he didn't sleep at night—and preparing himself for the following night, they cut down the tree where he had his lookout. The tree fell to the earth with such a loud boom that it sounded as if it had let out a groan. Cipollino didn't hear: he was sleeping tranquilly.

The people had gathered around to watch the spectacle and were waiting for him to wake up. Everyone was interested to see what he would do now that the tree with his observation platform was no longer there.

Yet nothing spectacular happened. Cipollino stood for a long time by the felled tree, looked up once at the sky, and then went and locked himself in his house.

At first, the village was laughing, but then we children

CIPOLLINO

began to miss Cipollino, and then the grown-ups did, too, and then Heaven and the Earth? Though why Heaven and Earth, if Heaven received his soul and the Earth his body? Yet for my fellow villagers, only the memory of Cipollino remained, of him who indeed could not cross into the kingdom of God, over the border of this domain whose boundary he had been able to cross on Earth.

He trusted his heart, full of love and kindness, and that is what made him do what nobody else in the village even dared.

FULL STOP AND COMMA

translated by Ollie Matthews

Everything on this earth has a name. As soon as we come into the world our family give us a name, then we walk around with this name for as long as we are fated to live under the sun, and then we pass on... we give ourselves to our Creator's blessing "in the name of the Father, the Son, and the Holy Spirit, now and forever, for the ages of ages".

No one knows what lies beyond, but here on this earth our name will remain. A name adorns a person, and a person adorns a name. Lord above, how many names I remember: Bataturi, Bezhia, Seba, Khvtiso, Ashekali, Nino, Guja—and how many more have walked upon the face of the earth and are no more, having passed along the fleeting path of life. It seems to me that I have forgotten their faces. I remember one time when Nino, the daughter of Sijana, came along the little path into the village. It was raining, and the mud was up to her knees.

FULL STOP AND COMMA

The Sijana woman had a little girl slung across her back, and to top it off she was bent double with age, and ambled along laboriously. She took cover in our shelter to catch her breath, and so as to make the neighbours hear she mumbled: "What good have I got out of this life? And now they've gone and named this girl after me!" Having said this, she dissolved into the rain and was seen no more.

How many, many wretched people have gone through their life bearing the sadness of their name…?

How many have had pet-names and nicknames added to their name?

How many have gone nameless?

How many are looking for a name?

And how many more lose their name?

And so on and so forth… I remember and then I remember no more, and the ones who stand out most vividly in my memory are Full Stop and Comma, two little girls whose real names nobody seemed to know (presumably they were named after their grandmothers). I don't know if it was their teachers or their schoolmates who called one of them Full Stop and the other Comma, but from then on they went to school as Full Stop and Comma.

They lived in a small abandoned mountain village. In the winter, smoke rose from the village in two places, and two lights could be seen flickering. This small village was connected to the world by three threads of hope: the smoke, which wafted lethargically up to the sky; the lights that flickered in the windows at night; and the two little girls, who every morning at dawn set out from the village and with their satchels slung on their backs ran down the slope. The school

FULL STOP AND COMMA

was very far away. They reached a little grove where the bus stopped, and there they took the bus to school; this bus alone, single-handedly, connected this god-forsaken valley to the outside world. The bus had to go all the way down to Tbilisi, come up again and go back down again, and so the pupils would gather at the roadside every morning at first light to go to school.

Whenever I had to take this bus, I would be witness to such scenes:

It is morning. Full Stop and Comma come sliding down the snow-covered slopes on their school bags. Full Stop in front, Comma behind. Full Stop gets stuck in the snow, and Comma is yanking on her arms to pull her out. The bus arrives, and all the passengers are waiting for Full Stop and Comma. Comma somehow manages to free Full Stop from the snow, and they run to catch the bus. Full Stop is first onto the bus, followed by Comma, and then they will get off the bus at school in the same order.

It is snowing. There they go, walking back up to the village, Full Stop in front, Comma behind.

It is raining. Full Stop is walking in front, Comma behind. Comma is holding an umbrella, and they both huddle under it.

Full Stop and Comma were never seen apart. It was said that their teacher would call Full Stop up to the blackboard for recital first, and then Comma. I think they were used to their nicknames. Once I deliberately asked them what their names were, and of course Full Stop answered for them both: "My name is Full Stop, and hers is Comma."

"Don't you get annoyed that they call you Full Stop and Comma?"

FULL STOP AND COMMA

"Who cares what they call us? There's one kid in year eight that they call Square Root, and he gets annoyed."

"Don't you get annoyed?"

"No. What's the use of getting annoyed? We are just fine as Full Stop and Comma," Full Stop told me, and their faces glowed with warmth. Then I thought to myself I had better stop there.

From that time on, the road had known several different buses. This small village, clinging to the side of the mountain and practically abandoned, was for a long time connected to the outside world by only three threads of hope: smoke crawled up towards the sky, lights flickered in the windows in the evening, and Full Stop and Comma went off to school.

Time passed.

They grew up.

They were married.

First Full Stop, then Comma.

Full Stop's husband was tall and looked like an exclamation mark.

Comma's husband was forever on the go: he could not sit still.

You can picture the scene: Full Stop comes to stay at her father's house; coming up the slope behind her, carrying the suitcases is Exclamation Mark, and behind him follow little Full Stops.

I also see Comma from time to time, making her way up to the village, but her husband is forever on the go and he runs on ahead. I am not sure why I cannot make out any little Commas: maybe they have not been born yet, maybe they are as restless as their father, and they have already gone up the

FULL STOP AND COMMA

slope to their grandparents'.

No one knows what will come next, or what will change this picture. Maybe the time will come for the smoke to stop, for the bright flickering in the windows during the evenings to stop, and for these little Full Stops and Commas to stop walking up and down this path. Lord above, give mercy to all our names upon this earth, do not drop your full stops and commas, and don't lead us into temptation, in the glory of Thy name.

NINE QUESTIONS ABOUT LOVE

translated by Clifford Marcus

1

"Excuse me. What is your name?"
"Gocha."
"Surname?"
"Chopikashvili."
"How old are you, Gocha?"
"Sixteen."
"Have you got someone you're in love with?"
"In love with?"
"Yes, what's the matter? Why are you laughing?"
"Dunno…"
"What's her name?"

NINE QUESTIONS ABOUT LOVE

"Who?"

"The girl you're in love with."

"I don't know."

"How come? Don't you know her name?"

"No, I only saw her once and that was from a long way away."

"What do you think: what is love?"

"Who knows? I guess wanting someone forever…"

2

"Marta Pirveli."

"Oh, what a beautiful name you have!"

"Indeed!"

"I really like it."

"Thank you!"

"Marta, can I ask you some questions about love, if that's all right with you?"

"Sure, go ahead, on the contrary I really like talking about love."

"Ok, if that's the case, tell me honestly are you in love with someone?"

"No, I'm married!"

3

"What is your name?"
"My name?"
"Yes."
"Kola, Nikolozi. They call me Nikipore."
"Which one do you prefer?"
"Me? Niko."
"And what would your surname be?"
"Chukurtmishvili, Nikipore Chukurtmishvili."
"Do you have a wife and children?"
"One son by my first wife, he's in the army now, I'm waiting for a letter from him. From the second wife a son and a daughter, the younger one is in year eight, the older one is in year ten. The girl is better in school, the boy doesn't do anything in school, that doesn't matter... it's better for a boy that way, any job will make a man of him. I was like that too, wasn't I? But the third wife didn't produce any children, but what can you do? You can't kick her out, I can't do anything about it, her brothers are like cannibals."

"So tell me, what is love?"

"Haven't you heard? Fear is father to love, that's for sure. What can I do? She went childless on me. But she had these brothers, just like cannibals, I love her, what else can I do? My hands are tied, there's nothing I can do about it."

NINE QUESTIONS ABOUT LOVE

"What would you say about loving your children?"
"May their father love them!"
"But you do see them, don't you?"
"No, I send them child support."

4

"What year are you in, Lado?"
"I'll be in year four."
"What are your marks like?"
"Dunno!"
"A girl in your class told me you might only be getting twos. Is that right?"
"No way!"
"So, what are your marks?"
"Five, four, now and then the odd three."
"What's your surname?"
"Tsiklauri."
"So you must have a girlfriend?"
"No way have I got a girlfriend!"
"So why did they tell me you have got a girlfriend?"
"It's not true."
"Is she your classmate?"
"Who?"
"The girl you're in love with."
"I'm not in love with anyone."

"So why did they tell me?"

"What did they tell you?"

"Lado loves the girl who sits behind him in class."

"Not the one behind me, the one in front," Lado blurted out and blushed as he hung his head in embarrassment.

5

"What can I tell you about love? I'm past the age for that."

"What age?"

"The age when you can believe that love really exists."

"You mean that…"

"Yeah yeah, before I used to believe it exists, but it was probably all a childish illusion."

"Then how did you guess that it doesn't exist?"

"Quite simple, when we finished school we separated. I carried on studying and he went into the army."

"Then?"

"Then I married one of my fellow students."

"So you weren't in love with him?"

"You sound just like my husband."

"Why?"

"She loves me, she loves me not, it's just words, the main thing is a simple understanding, right?"

"How does this simple understanding show itself?"

"I suppose in a lot of things, at least he doesn't have to ask me all kinds of stuff, like where I've been, why I'm late, every last little thing, does he?"

"That depends."

"Like I said, right?"

"What did you say?"

"When I said you talk just like my ex-husband."

"You're not going to get back together?"

"Who with, the one I went to school with?"

"I'm sorry."

"It's all right."

"One more question: if you met the first one again and he wanted to rekindle the old flame, what would you do?"

"Who are you talking about?"

"About the one you were in school with, I suppose he's back from the army now."

"So you mean Gocha? He even came to see me, when he found out I was separated from my husband, he went on and on saying how he can't live without me."

"Then what did you tell him?"

"I said I'd think about it. That was on 29th January. We agreed to meet on 29th February and I would give him my answer. I deliberately didn't give him my address, he knew the old address, but we had moved. If any of our mutual friends knew my new address, I just warned them not to tell him."

"Why?"

"Because I was wondering if I was really in love or not. If I really loved him, I wouldn't be able to stop myself seeing him on 29th February. I didn't want to see him before then, do you understand? I was testing myself."

"What did you find out?"

NINE QUESTIONS ABOUT LOVE

"That year there were twenty-eight days in February, not twenty-nine."

"So you didn't meet?"

"I went on the 28th February and 1st March."

"He didn't come?"

"I bumped into him not long ago and you know what he said? 'I'm sorry, I had something very important on 29th and I couldn't make it.' Then I realized it had just been a childish crush."

"So you don't believe in love?"

"No way."

"And what kind of love would you like?"

"Of course, I'd just like there to be mutual understanding."

6

"Grandmother, can I ask you something?"

"What, my child?"

"What is love?"

"Aren't you love? Love is the person in front of you."

NINE QUESTIONS ABOUT LOVE

7

"My name is Apollo."

"Last name?"

"Mghebrishvili."

"Where do you work?"

"There."

"What do you mean by 'there'?"

"What do you need to know for?"

"If you had to, could you give your life for love?"

"What me? For a woman, are you kidding me? Love is not the kind of thing that's worth dying for."

8

"Young people today? They don't care about shame or honour. 'We are in love,' they say. They just hang around each other's necks and snog. They don't even look at you. It makes no difference whether you're watching them or not: they say they love each other and that's it! Then what? Did we behave the way these modern couples go on in public? So does that mean we didn't love each other? Do they have a different love because they are educated? I would shake all over like I don't know what whenever I saw my husband. I didn't dare show it, I couldn't even call him by his name in public I was so shy. He went to the grave and I never even looked him in the eye. With young people today they almost devour each other with their eyes.

It makes you sick, I don't believe in that kind of love. Say what you want, but I don't believe in it."

9

Ninth and last question, and why is it the last? Have we learned anything from the previous answers? You can ask as many questions about the nature of love as there are people in the world. Every answer to the question 'What is love?' will be the right one. It will be right because everyone looks at it in their own way. But it will still be unfathomable because the nature of love is always unfathomable and changing.

Isn't that right?

Everyone has to try to find their own answer to this question: "But all the same what is love? What is it like? Could you live without it?"

Our story could go on forever like this and never get to the heart of the matter.

And if someone insists on answering back: "Prove that

NINE QUESTIONS ABOUT LOVE

love exists."

There is only one answer: love is like this: it doesn't need to prove itself. It proves itself wherever it sets foot.

THE COMMUNAL CROW

translated by Ollie Matthews

"Surname!"

"Chokheli."

"First name!"

"Butula..."

"Profession?"

"Village priest."

"Who is your complaint about?"

"The Shughlians' boy, Makhara. You know, the one everyone calls Ghvtisavari."

"What's the problem?"

"The problem is my crow's been taken away from me. They've turned him against me and they're saying, 'he's ours now'—and they won't give him back."

"What do you mean, your crow? Are you having me on?"

"Everyone knew he was my crow. I used to take him

everywhere with me, into the hayfields, the meadows… he was mine, and now they've turned him against me."

"Wait, wait… so you had a pet crow? What was its name?"

"The crow?"

"Yes, the crow."

"Nothing, people just called him Butula's crow."

"So, you didn't give him a name. Understood."

"What do you mean, understood?"

"That you took this crow into your personal possession?"

"As God is my witness… I…"

"God? You dare to utter that word in here!"

"Forgive me… it's just…"

"Citizen Butula, how long did you have this crow in your personal possession?"

"Nine years, sir."

"Why won't they give him back?"

"They say he belongs to them."

"Who does the crow wish to belong to?"

"They bribed the crow, sir, they bring him bird seed day and night. He always flies over to them."

"They don't have a name for it either?"

"No, they don't."

Butula and the judge discussed the affair of the crow late into the night. When finally he went home, the village priest was so tired he had a job not to fall off his horse.

"How did it go, what did he say? 'I will make them compensate you for the loss of the crow'? Spit it out. What are you staring at?" his wife kept asking him.

"He said we were both guilty. First I took the crow for my own, now Makhara's taken him. He's accusing us of having ulterior motives."

"Yes, but did he say anything about compensation?"

"All he said about money was, I might have to cough up a hundred roubles."

"Whatever for?"

"He says tomorrow morning we're to go up to the village to run a little test. Up on a rooftop I'm to put down some bird seed on one side and Makhara will do the same on the other side. We'll stand next to the bird seed we've put down and the judge will stand in the middle, then we'll wait for the crow. If he flies to my side then Makhara will pay a fine of a hundred roubles, if he flies to Makhara's side then I will pay."

"Have you lost your mind? This last Saints' Day the villagers donated no more than a hundred roubles, and you're going to spend it on a fine!? You know it'll fly to the other chap."

"But what can I do?"

The next morning the whole village surrounded the Shughlians' rooftop. Makhara stood on one side of the rooftop, Butula on the other, and in between them loomed the judge. Half of the village was rooting for Butula and the other half for Makhara. It all came down to the crow. But they were kept waiting, as for some reason the crow was in no rush to get the show started.

The judge started to suspect he was being made a fool of. But looking at Makhara's and Butula's daft faces he started to get hopeful and he reproached himself for not setting the fine at two hundred roubles.

Then suddenly the crowd got excited. The crow appeared in the air, turned circles in the clouds, and glided gracefully

THE COMMUNAL CROW

towards them. Before he flew down, Makhara's and Butula's hearts were in their mouths.

Finally he swooped down low over their heads, his wings cracked, and he landed on the judge's hat, whereupon he screeched, shat all over it, then flew away.

Makhara and Butula breathed a sigh of relief: "We've dodged the fine!"

But the judge didn't let up easily, he soon realised what was happening and accused Makhara and Butula again.

"On account of your ulterior motives in taking the crow for your own and since you didn't give it a name, moreover, for moral indecency, both of you are obliged to pay a fine of two hundred roubles each, otherwise you will be prosecuted. You have one week."

The judge cleaned his hat, put it back on, and went away. Makhara was worried about where he was going to find the two hundred roubles. Butula however had reason for hope: before the last Saints' Day a hundred roubles had been donated at the shrine, now in two days' time there was another Saints' Day and there would probably be another one hundred roubles.

But disaster struck: fewer people came on the Saints' Day and Butula collected fewer donations than he had expected. Nor was Makhara able to raise the money in a week, for as soon as people knew what he needed it for they wouldn't give him anything. They closed the door and grumbled to themselves: "Go look at the crows and maybe they will drop money on you."

A week later the judge summoned both of them and wouldn't let them go home. The whole day they called in witnesses from the village for questioning. They were seeking

THE COMMUNAL CROW

to establish the identity of the crow.

Some people managed to get out of going to court; at the first questioning they silently slipped the judge some money, then on the way back to the village they proudly boasted to the villagers who had already been in for questioning eight times.

The village had had enough. They put together four hundred roubles and took it to the judge in order to secure their fellow-villagers' release.

The judge tapped his fingers on the table, and dissatisfied, dumped the money in a drawer. The village elders despaired.

"I will satisfy your request on the condition that you catch the crow and bring him here to me personally, alive."

Big and small alike went out searching for the crow. But the crow kept his distance. He rarely flew down to the village; usually he would just alight on a tree, caw, then fly off again. The villagers couldn't catch him, but they couldn't kill him either. The judge had said, "Bring him back to me alive," and if they killed him then the whole village might be fined.

Finally, Gamikhardai had an idea.

"There's no way the judge would recognise whether it was the same crow or another one!"

"He won't be able to tell the difference."

"So let's catch a different crow and take that one to him."

"He's right."

"But what if he does recognise the crow?" Some people were doubtful.

"Dear neighbours, how would he remember it at first glance? Besides, I don't think he even saw the crow when it landed on his hat and flew away."

"Very well, but what if Butula and Makhara let slip that it

THE COMMUNAL CROW

isn't the same crow, then what would we do then?"

"Let's send a man to them to warn them what we're doing and not to blurt anything out."

They sent a man to Butula and Makhara to warn them.

There was an old crow who kept a nest in the village's fruit trees. There were always little chicks hatching in the nest, and the villagers were so accustomed to them that they never bothered them. The old crow looked on them with goodwill, and it was unheard of for someone to catch a nestling.

There was no other way. The people decided to take this crow to the judge. They sent children up the tree and they brought down the crow still sitting in her nest.

Poor crow, who had forever been convinced of the people's kindness, she didn't even put up a fight. When they brought her down, the women sang their typical lament:

"Woe! Your poor babies!"

"Alas! Her babies are left to fend for themselves!"

"It's us who ought to be troubled, for as they say crows live for three hundred years. Hopefully before then the judge will have died and she will be free again."

"Not three hundred, more like sixty!"

"No, woman, you don't get it, three hundred."

"Maybe he himself doesn't know and that's why he said to bring the crow alive, so he can see how long she lives for."

"But the poor babies are left all alone!"

"The ravens won't let this chance slip!"

"Oh yes, woman!"

The poor crow must have sensed something was wrong, for she screeched as they took her away.

The judge kept his promise to the people: he let Butula

THE COMMUNAL CROW

and Makhara go. On their way out Butula turned to the judge again and whispered in his ear:

"Don't tell anyone I told you, but… they gave you a different crow."

"What do you mean, a different crow?" asked the judge indignantly and stormed outside.

"Either you bring me the crow alive, or you will be fined for lying to me!"

What could the villagers do? They all looked sad as they came away. To this day they're still searching for the crow but can't find him anywhere.

Thus they lament: "If she isn't going to live for three hundred years, we would already have a document proving she grew old and died."

They're still searching everywhere.

Butula doesn't have to worry about any of this. He died an old man.

AFTERWORD

The history, the characters, a few choice dramatic episodes—you have just been on a tour of the Gudamaqari Gorge. You have met locals with quirky names and learnt about their customs; day has passed into night, into winter. After the curtain falls and the characters go home, the mountains still stand all around. There is no getting away from them, or going beyond them.

Chokheli was not just a masterful writer, he was a decorated filmmaker. His stories and films dovetail to create a long, unified oeuvre dedicated to the life and times of his native place. Typically his films open and end with long panning shots going up and down the valley. In common with the stories, they place the Gudamaqari Gorge front and centre as

AFTERWORD

an imaginative space, as a present, participating protagonist in his characters' lives.

Born in 1954, Goderdzi Chokheli grew up in the village of Chokhi in the Gudamaqari Gorge, attending the village primary school and completing his secondary education in the nearby town of Pasanauri. In 1972 he went to Tbilisi to attend the Shota Rustaveli Theatre and Georgia State Film University where he studied in the Faculty of Film Studies and the Faculty of Film Directing. After graduation in 1979 he was accepted as a production director at the Georgian Film Studio. From 1980 he was a member of the Cinematographers' Union. At the same time, he started writing. His stories were published. Gudamaqari started to be shared with the world.

Director and diplomat Lana Ghoghoberidze, famed for her *The Day Is Longer Than the Night* (1984), describes her first impressions of Chokheli when he came up to study under her: "He came to the theatre institute straight from the Gudamaqari Gorge... a small, thin boy who didn't look at all like a stereotypical mountain person and immediately caught my attention with his observant gaze mature beyond his years, as well as his tendency to be silent and detached from others, and, most importantly, his God-given talent for writing."[12]

Chokheli was only in his third year when his short film, *Adgilis deda*, won the Grand Prize at the 1981 Oberhausen International Short Film Festival. Named after the "place-mother" or guardian angel associated with each locality in the

---

12   Ghoghoberidze, L., *Rats megoneba da rogorts megoneba*. Bakur Sulakauri Publishing House, 2020, p. 110

AFTERWORD

Gudamaqari Gorge, this simple but haunting tableau presents an elderly woman going about her menial daily tasks before deciding to take her own life. The perilous climax of the film has the woman putting her head in a noose repeatedly, each time interrupting herself to attend to another little task. Finally, her cow returns, and the woman must milk her. We are left with the sense that the mundane, repetitive life of the mountains will endure forever. According to Ghoghoberidze, who was a jury member at the festival, the film moved the audience to laughter and tears. She goes on to write that: "The little boy Goderdzi met his success with silent joy and philosophical calm."

The boy from the mountains who grew up to become an internationally decorated film director brought his native valley to the world. Whether Gudamaqari owes more to Chokheli, or Chokheli more to Gudamaqari is not an original question to ask.[13] What is not in doubt is the role played by the gorge as artistic backdrop. Chokheli saw it himself as an arena for the world's drama to be played out: if, he writes in his novel *Human Sadness* (1984), "the Earth is the paper of [a] great book which is called 'the World'", then "Gudamaqari Gorge is another, the subtitle for countless short stories".[14]

Chokheli's formula seems to be the combining of the grave with the absurd. An early work, *The Khevsurian from Bakhurkhevi* (1980), portrays a young man bored with the monotony of life who decides to have fun by scaring his fellow villagers with his gun and forcing the old women to

---

13 https://www.radiotavisupleba.ge/a/ამერიკაი-ზაზა-ბურჯულაძე-გოდერძი-ჩოხელზე/33132380.html, (accessed 22nd April 2025)
14 Chokheli, G., *Human Sadness*. Dedalus, 2024

AFTERWORD

play football. In the end, accidentally, the gun is turned on himself.

An example of a later, feature-length work is *The Gospel According to Luke* (1998), which won the prize of the best script at that year's Kinoshok festival. In this more conventional narrative, a village boy (played by Chokheli's son, Luka Chokheli) is punished by his schoolteacher for possessing a book of the Gospels. He is symbolically crucified by his schoolmates: forced to carry a wooden cross used to uphold a scarecrow and mocked in an act reminiscent of Christ on the road to Calvary.

Whatever the plot of the films, they are peppered with naturalistic detail: in most scenes, characters are performing some sort of menial task, and the mountains of the Gudamaqari Gorge are visible in almost every shot. The constant presence of the mountains brings them into the centre, making them witnesses to the action, if not active protagonists. It becomes apparent that the Gorge is a key subject of his art.

In these stories from Chokheli's world, we—his fortunate audience—can see ourselves and our own world as we hold it to be true.

Our own world as we hold it to be true—we know from lived experience that it is frequently incoherent, surreal, that actually there is no narrative. Chokheli's realism is the realism of our own lives.

In his 1981 short film, *Mekvle*, he does away with narrative altogether. The entire film plays out as a montage of winter scenes from Gudamaqari, overlayed with audio of families celebrating the new year together. The word "*mekvle*" can be translated as "first foot" and refers to the first guest to enter

AFTERWORD

the house in the new year. A version of the film with revised English subtitles has been prepared by members of the Oxford Georgian Translation Project, and was shown at the Bologna Short Film Festival in 2018 and again at the opening of the London International Film Festival in 2019.

In the absence of a clear narrative, we might consider *Mekvle* a work of ethnography: a recording of voices that is more documentary in nature than, say, a Georgian re-imagining of *Under Milk Wood*. It is a work that blurs the fictional and the non-fictional.

Such is true of *Human Sadness* (1984), his screen adaptation of his eponymous novel, which was translated by the Oxford Georgian Translation Project in 2024. In a departure from his earlier films, he introduces elements of the supernatural, making use of digitally enhanced effects to depict the flying severed head of a goat.

As the academic Vakhtang Guruli put it in his essay "The Righteous Goderdzi": "In the world of Goderdzi Chokheli, the line between people, animals, birds, plants was erased. All of them are integral parts of one whole; their main rule is to exist as one and in harmony. Goderdzi Chokheli erased the distinction between worldly and otherworldly, between life and death, between 'to be human' and 'not to be human.'"[15]

The interaction between the films and literature in Chokheli's oeuvre is not limited to screen adaptations of his own stories. To watch a Chokheli film and then to start reading a story can feel rather synonymous. To a certain extent, his stories can be watched. His technique of picking out a few key details

---

15 Guruli, V., "Righteous Chokheli", Universali, Tbilisi, 2020

AFTERWORD

and mentioning them repeatedly throughout a story, such as the smoke trails in the distance in "Full Stop and Comma", recall his directing style in the films. Parallels abound between characters' philosophical struggles: the protagonist of "Fish Letters" deciding to renounce his life as a human recalls themes of abandonment and suicide in his first film. Here again, his realism teeters on the edge of the absurd. As in the films, he is adept at doing away with narrative structure altogether: in the question-and-answer format of "Nine Questions About Love", in which we do not "see" the characters, he manages to paint distinctive pen portraits through dialogue alone.

What is really astonishing, and what is perhaps Chokheli's highest merit, is his ability to capture in a few pages of prose, or in fifteen minutes of film, vast universal dramas. His beguilingly straightforward plots capture a sense of the epic in the simple. In the story of Gudamaqari he manages to tell the story of the world.

Today the Gudamaqari Gorge is little changed from how it appears in Chokheli's works. I was fortunate enough to go there in the summer of 2024, and I was surprised, and then unsurprised, to find that on this face on which time makes but little impression people are living in much the same way. I stayed with Chokheli's stepmother, who lives up in the mountains in the summer. She tends to her cows, collects water from a stream, makes delicious cheese, and spends a lot of the day staring out across the valley. I always wondered what she saw that was new.

Sadly Chokheli is no longer with us. The world lost this

AFTERWORD

"uncommon genius"[16] in 2007. I was struck by how fondly the villagers I met spoke of him. In fact, his presence was palpable. I had the distinct sense that translating his words, and then dining with his family, is probably about as close as you can get to a dead man. One relative relayed to me how a grandmother was able to speak with the birds. She invented a different language to speak to them and they always answered her and came to sit with her. This struck me as perfectly plausible. If you read a few pages of Chokheli, or watch one of his films, it will not seem unbelievable to you that a woman in the last century devised her own language to communicate with birds.

The old primary school in the village of Chokhi is being converted into a museum dedicated to Chokheli's life and work. His desk with its lifting lid and inkwell still stands in its place. I ran my hands over it. When he sat here in the most forgettable class of the most forgettable day of his childhood, his talent was already alive in him. He saw his classmates and his teacher with the same eyes through which, decades later, he would observe and immortalise his native land.

In his art, Chokheli captured everything that went into him. His art stands as a monument to this everything. The greatest artists, I find, inspire feelings of gratitude. Perhaps this is the ultimate triumph. I showed a man a copy of our English translation of *Human Sadness*. His face lit up and he took a photo of it and sent it to somebody on Messenger. Then he told me how he and everyone loved Chokheli, about what Chokheli had done for their community, about his plans for the museum, his ambitions for it.

Ollie Matthews

---

16 Berdzenishvili, L., "An Unacknowledged Saint"

FILMOGRAPHY

- *Adgilis deda* (1976)
- The Khevsurian from Bakhurkhevi (1980)
- *Mekvle* (1981)
- Human Sadness (1984)
- A Letter to Spruce Trees (1986)
- Easter Lamb (1988)
- The Stranger (1988)
- White Flag (1989)
- Children of Sin (1989)
- Doves of Paradise (1997)
- The Gospel According to Luke (1998)
- Chained Knights (1999)
- Fire of Love (2003)

AWARDS

- Grand Prize for the film "*Adgilis deda*", International Short Film Festival Oberhausen (1981)
- "Silver Nymph" and prize of International Catholic Church for the film "Children of Sin", Monte Carlo Film Festival (1991)
- Special Prize at Japan Film Festival, Hiroshima, for "Children of Sin" (1991)
- Prizes for the Best Script and Best Film Producing at Tbilisi "Gold Eagle" Festival for "Children of Sin" (1992)
- Grand Prize at "Kinoshok" Open Film Festival of CIS and Baltic countries, Anapa, for the film "Doves of Paradise" (1997)
- Prize for the best script at "Kinoshok" Open Film Festival of CIS and Baltic countries, Anapa, for the film "The Gospel According to Luke" (1998)

BIBLIOGRAPHY

- *Letter to the Fir Trees* – 1980
- *Twilight Valley* – 1981
- *Human Sadness* – 1984
- *The Wolf* – 1988
- *Fish Letters* – 1989
- *The Priest's Sin* – 1990
- *Save Me, Mother Earth* – 1991
- *The Life of Grass* – 1997

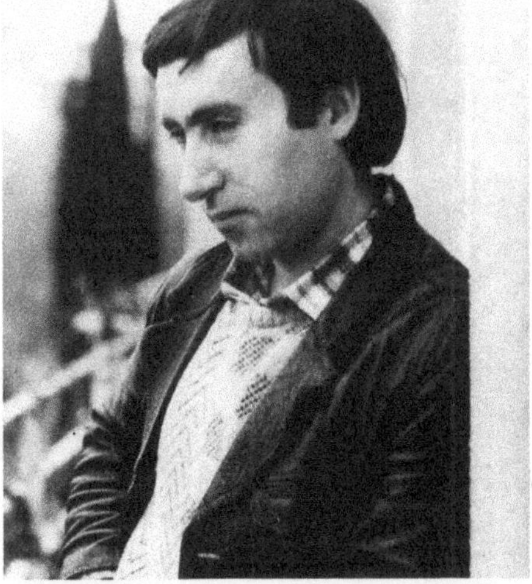

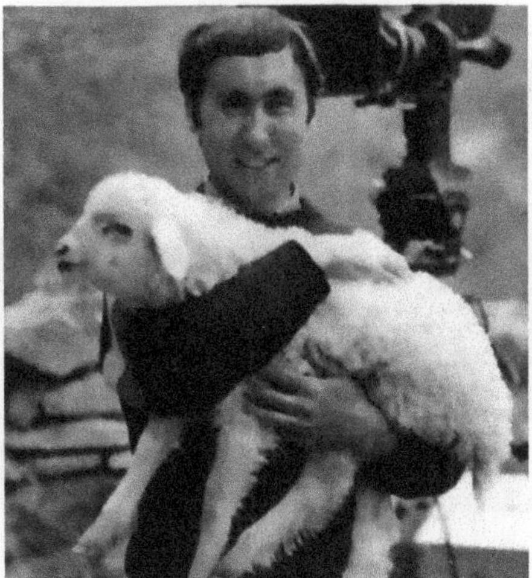

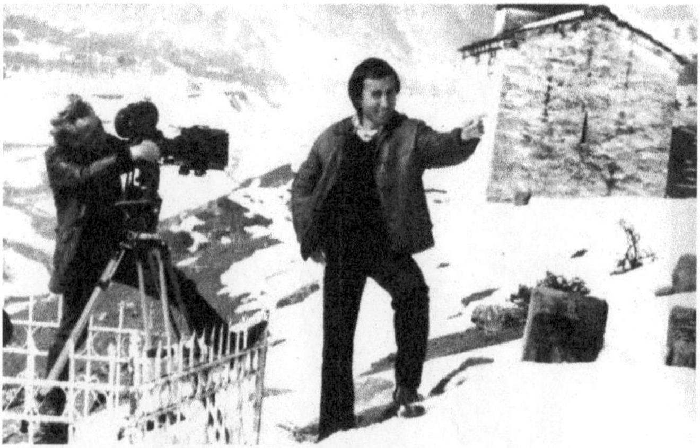

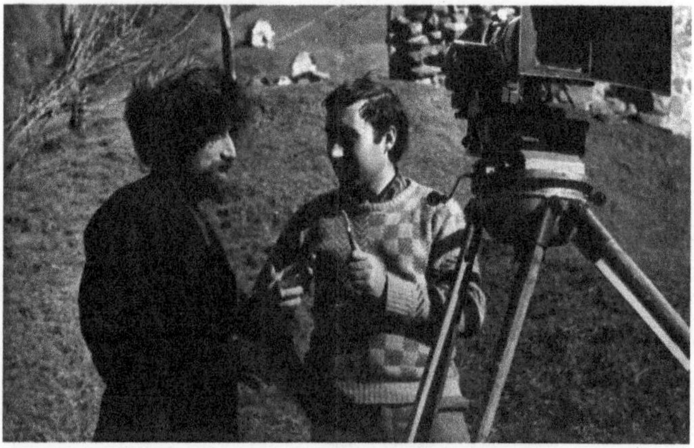